W9-BUR-608

THE

Good-Night Kiss

Atheneum
Macmillan Publishing Company
866 Third Avenue
New York, NY 10022

Maxwell Macmillan Canada, Inc.
1200 Eglinton Avenue East
Suite 200
Don Mills, Ontario M3C 3N1

Macmillan Publishing Company is part of
the Maxwell Communication Group of Companies.

First edition

Printed in Hong Kong by South China Printing Company (1988) Ltd.

10 9 8 7 6 5 4 3 2 1

The text of this book is set in 14 pt. Century Schoolbook.

Library of Congress Cataloging-in-Publication Data

Aylesworth, Jim.
    The good-night kiss/by Jim Aylesworth.—1st ed.
        p.   cm.
    Summary: The nighttime world includes lots of quiet activity,
from animals moving in the woods to cars on the city streets to a
child hearing a bedtime story and receiving a good-night kiss.
    ISBN 0-689-31515-5
    [1. Night—Fiction. 2. Bedtime—Fiction.] I. Title.
PZ7.A983Go   1993
[E]—dc20   91-40952

THE
*G*ood-Night Kiss

by Jim Aylesworth

illustrated by Walter Lyon Krudop

ATHENEUM   1993   NEW YORK

Maxwell Macmillan Canada
Toronto

Maxwell Macmillan International
New York Oxford Singapore Sydney

For those who tuck them in, with love!
— JA

To my grandparents
— WLK

On the night of the good-night kiss, a small green frog peeks out from under a lily pad.

And when that small green frog peeks out from under that lily pad, it sees an old raccoon sniffing along the pond bank, looking for something to eat.

And when that old raccoon climbs over the trunk of a fallen cottonwood tree, it sees a deer drinking from the moon-lit water.

And when that deer walks back up across the meadow, it sees an owl flying toward an old red barn on the other side of a field.

And when that owl lands on the open haymow door of that old barn, it sees a farmer climbing down from the seat of a great green tractor.

And when that farmer crosses the barnyard on his way back to the house, he sees a man in a rusty pickup truck driving down the dusty gravel road.

And when that man in the pickup truck pulls in to a gas station out on the highway, he sees a man in a huge silver eighteen-wheeler coming to a stop at a red light.

And when that truck driver passes beneath a railroad bridge, he sees a man in the window of a caboose at the end of a long freight train.

And when that man in the caboose passes through the next town, he sees a man walking his dog along a darkened street of small stores and shops.

And when that man with the dog comes to the next corner,
he sees a woman in a blue car come to a stop at a stop sign.

And when that woman in the blue car crosses the tracks and turns onto a quiet, tree-lined street, she sees a cat out walking across the grass.

And when that cat passes by a rosebush at the side of a house, it sees a snow white moth flutter up to the light coming from an upstairs window.

And when that snow white moth lands on the screen of that lighted window, it sees a young child lying in a cozy bed and a person who loves that child reading that child a storybook.

And when that person who loves that child turns the last page in that storybook, that person leans over and gives that child a kiss good night.

"Good night!"